Teachers, librarians, and kids from across Canada are talking about the *Canadian Flyer Adventures.* Here's what some of them had to say:

I love the fact that these are Canadian adventures—kids should know how exciting Canadian history is. Emily and Matt are regular kids, full of curiosity, and I can see readers relating to them. ~ *JEAN K., TEACHER, ONTARIO*

## What kids told us:

I would like to have the chance to ride on a magical sled and have adventures. ~ *EMMANUEL*

I would like to tell the author that her book is amazing, incredible, awesome, and a million times better than any book I've read. ~ *MARIA*

I would recommend the *Canadian Flyer Adventures* series to other kids so they could learn about Canada too. The book is just the right length and hard to put down. ~ *PAUL*

The books I usually read are the full-of-fact encyclopedias. This book is full of interesting ideas that simply grab me. ~ *ELEANOR*

At the end of the book Matt and Emily say they are going on another adventure. I'm very interested in where they are going next! ~ *ALEX*

I like when Emily and Matt fly into the sky on a sled towards a new adventure. I can't wait for the next book! ~ *JI SANG*

# Arctic Storm

## Frieda Wishinsky

Illustrated by Patricia Ann Lewis-MacDougall

For my friend Mary Courneyea

Many thanks to the hard-working Owlkids team, for their insightful comments and steadfast support. Special thanks to Patricia Ann Lewis-MacDougall and Barb Kelly for their engaging and energetic illustrations and design.

Maple Tree books are published by Owlkids Books Inc.
10 Lower Spadina Avenue, Suite 400, Toronto, Ontario  M5V 2Z2
www.owlkids.com

Text © 2011 Frieda Wishinsky
Illustrations © 2011 Patricia Ann Lewis-MacDougall

Library and Archives Canada Cataloguing in Publication

Wishinsky, Frieda
Arctic storm / Frieda Wishinsky ; illustrated by Patricia Ann Lewis-MacDougall.

(Canadian flyer adventures ; 16)
Issued also in electronic format.
ISBN 978-1-926818-09-2 (bound).--ISBN 978-1-926818-10-8 (pbk.)

I. Lewis-MacDougall, Patricia Ann  II. Title.  III. Series: Wishinsky, Frieda.
Canadian flyer adventures ; 16.

PS8595.I834A73 2011          jC813'.54          C2011-900257-4

Library of Congress Control Number:  2010943319

E-book ISBN: 978-1-926818-17-7

Canada Council    Conseil des Arts          ONTARIO ARTS COUNCIL
for the Arts       du Canada                CONSEIL DES ARTS DE L'ONTARIO

We acknowledge the financial support of the Canada Council for the Arts, the Ontario Arts Council, the Government of Canada through the Canada Book Fund (CBF), and the Government of Ontario through the Ontario Media Development Corporation's Book Initiative for our publishing activities.

Manufactured by Friesens Corporation
Manufactured in Altona, MB, Canada in March 2011
Job# 64280

A          B          C          D          E          F

# CONTENTS

# HOW IT ALL BEGAN

Emily and Matt couldn't believe their luck. They discovered an old dresser full of strange objects in the tower of Emily's house. They also found a note from Emily's Great-Aunt Miranda: "The sled is yours. Fly it to wonderful adventures."

They found a sled right behind the dresser! When they sat on it, shimmery gold words appeared:

*Rub the leaf*
*Three times fast.*
*Soon you'll fly*
*To the past.*

The sled rose over Emily's house. It flew over their town of Glenwood. It sailed out of a cloud and into the past. Their adventures on the flying sled had begun! Where will the sled take them next? Turn the page to find out.

# 1

# Woof

"Woof!"

Emily looked up from her book. A big black-and-white dog was pulling her friend Matt toward the porch.

"Whose dog is that?" called Emily.

Before Matt could answer, the dog bounded up the steps with Matt behind him. "It's my f...friend J...Jack's dog," stammered Matt, out of breath. "His name is Tiny."

"Tiny? Right, and my name is Cleopatra," said Emily. "No dog that big could be called Tiny."

"That's what Jack calls him," said Matt. He tried tying Tiny's leash to the railing, but Tiny jumped up and licked Emily's nose and cheeks.

"Well, at least he's friendly," said Emily. She patted the big dog's head. "He's soft, too."

"He likes you a lot," said Matt. "As soon as he saw you, he charged up to your porch."

Tiny sprawled out beside Emily. She rubbed the dog's ears as Matt tied his leash to the railing.

"What kind of dog is he?" Emily asked.

"Part Canadian Inuit and part Husky. Jack said that Inuit dogs are almost extinct, and he was lucky to adopt him."

"So, what are you doing with Tiny?"

"Jack and his family have to pick up his aunt at the airport. Tiny hates car rides. He tries to leap out of the car. Jack asked me to watch him till one o'clock."

"I once read a book about Inuit dogs," said Emily. "They're great at hauling sleds with people and supplies. Famous explorers like Roald Amundsen used them in the Arctic. Sled dogs can really run fast."

"No kidding," said Matt, flopping down on a chair beside Emily. "It's fun when he starts to run, but scary, too. I thought I was going to fall flat on the sidewalk."

"I bet it would be amazing to race a dogsled through the snow. I've always wanted to do that."

Matt nodded. "Me, too. You know…"

Emily's eyes sparkled. "I was thinking the same thing. After you take Tiny back, let's check the tower. You never know. There might be a dogsled adventure waiting for us there."

Matt looked at his watch.

"Wow! It's almost one o'clock. I'd better take

Tiny home. I'll be back soon. Jack only lives two blocks away."

"Great. I'll meet you here."

Matt untied the dog's leash. "Come on, Tiny," he said, giving the leash a little pull. But Tiny wouldn't move.

"Come *on!*" said Matt louder. But Tiny still wouldn't move. He licked Emily's hand.

"He doesn't want to leave you," said Matt.

Emily sighed. "I guess I'd better leave him, then. But he's such a sweet dog."

Emily patted Tiny's head again. Then she stood up and dashed inside. She peeked out the window as Matt tried to convince Tiny to move.

"Come on, Tiny," said Matt. "Emily's gone. Let's go see Jack."

Suddenly, as if he understood, Tiny pulled himself up and raced down the steps, dragging Matt behind him.

# 2

# Tricky

Matt was soon back on Emily's porch.

"Ready to mush?" she asked.

Matt laughed. "Ready."

Emily and Matt raced up the rickety back stairs to the tower room.

As soon as they were inside, Emily hurried over to the dresser. She peeked inside the first drawer.

"Nothing in the front. Nothing in the left corner. Nothing anywhere."

"Wait," said Matt. "I see something that

looks like a dog collar tucked way back in the right corner!" Matt lifted it out. "It *is* a dog collar and it says: *Moon Dog's collar, Yellowknife, 1976.* Yahoo! I think we've found our ticket to ride a dogsled!"

"So, what are we waiting for?" said Emily.

"I have my recorder. Do you have your sketchbook?"

"Yep. Right here," said Emily, patting the pocket of her jeans.

Emily pulled the sled out from behind the dresser. The two friends jumped on. As soon as they did, the magic words appeared:

> *Rub the leaf*
> *Three times fast.*
> *Soon you'll fly*
> *To the past.*

Matt rubbed the leaf on the front of the sled, and fog immediately surrounded them. When the sled lifted, they were flying over Emily's house and over Glenwood, and heading toward a fluffy white cloud.

"Too bad we couldn't take Tiny on the sled with us. He might have met his great-great-grandparents on this trip," said Emily.

"Yeah, right. Imagine taking a huge dog on the sled. We'd tip over for sure," said Matt.

"Maybe not," said Emily as they zoomed into the cloud. "Remember, our sled is magic."

Soon the sled burst out of the cloud.

"It's cold here," said Emily, with a shudder. She glanced down at her clothes. "Luckily we're wearing big fat parkas and warm boots and mittens."

"At least it's not snowing," said Matt.

"But there's already snow on the ground.

And look at the thick, grey clouds in the sky! I can feel the wind whip through my clothes. I bet a storm is on the way."

The sled flew lower and lower.

"Do you see any people?" asked Emily, peering around.

"Over there! I see people, dogs, and three sleds. Hooray! We are going to have a dogsled adventure!"

The magic sled touched down behind a tree.

"I hope no one saw us fly in. It's going to be tricky to explain what we're doing here. I thought we were landing in Yellowknife. It sure doesn't look like we're near a city. It looks more like we're in the middle of nowhere," said Matt.

"We can always say we're lost, which is true. We have no idea exactly where we are," Emily said.

Matt pulled the sled along the snow as they walked toward the group. As they neared, the dogs began to yelp and bark.

"Hey! Those dogs look a lot like Tiny," said Matt.

"And none of them are tiny, either. I wonder what they're called," said Emily.

A tall man with long brown hair pulled back into a ponytail looked up. Then he dashed over to Emily and Matt.

"Hey, you two! How did you get here? Where did you come from?"

# 3

# Storm Coming

"We're lost," said Emily.

"Lost? Did you kids wander off from your family? I bet you were on a dogsled trip, too." The man shook his head and wagged his finger at them. "Didn't your family warn you never to wander off, especially in the wilderness?"

"We know we shouldn't take off when we don't know where we're going, but we like adventures," Matt explained.

"How far have you wandered from your family?"

"Far," said Emily. "We're so glad to see you."

The man sighed. "I guess it is easy to get lost around here. We were supposed to meet our Inuit guides this morning, but then a heavy fog set in by midday. We've been wandering for hours and it's going to be dark soon."

Emily pointed to the sky. The clouds were thicker and darker now. "Do you think it's going to snow?"

"I think we're in for *something* big and maybe nasty. It's early in the fall for a snowstorm, but we've already had some snow. You never know around here. Bad weather can kick in quickly. Come on. Meet our group. I'm John Reed."

"I'm Matt and this is my friend Emily."

"Are you on a wilderness vacation?" asked Emily.

John laughed. "Not exactly. We've been studying caribou and wolf migration in the

Northwest Territories. This dogsled trip is a treat for my son, Arthur. We promised we'd take him after we completed all our scientific work. Who knew that a simple two-day adventure with dogsleds would turn out like this?"

"Wow! You're scientists," said Matt.

"Except for Arthur, of course. But we call him the junior scientist. He's only fifteen, but he's been a big help spotting animals for us. We camped north of Great Slave Lake for a month, tracking caribou and wolves. We also noted climate conditions. It was hard work. This part was supposed to be relaxing, and now we're lost like you."

The friends followed John to a spot near a forest where the group was gathered.

"So, who are these two?" said one of the scientists. He was the tallest of the group and had curly grey hair and a shaggy grey beard.

"This is Emily and Matt, Rob. They're lost."

Rob frowned. "That's all we need now. More kids. Your son is lying down on his sleeping bag behind your sled, John. He says he's not feeling well."

John sighed. "I'll see what's the matter with him. Meanwhile, over there fiddling with our radio is Sam Slade. He's the only one who knows how to fix our two-way radio. We need it to stay in touch."

Rob rolled his eyes. "I bet the radio is broken. We have no guides, a sick kid, two lost kids, a pack of hungry dogs, no working radio, and a storm coming. Why didn't those guides warn us more about this weather? Where are they, anyway? What else could go wrong?"

"Don't mind Rob Wiley," said John. "He's our official grouch. He read a scientific paper about global warming this year, and now he grumbles all the time that our climate is changing and we're all doomed. I keep telling him that we need to do something and let people know what's happening. It's no use just grumbling about it. Anyway, come on. Meet Sam and my son, Arthur. He probably ate something that didn't agree with him."

As they approached Arthur, they could see that his dark brown hair was matted with sweat. "I'm feeling a bit weird, Dad," he said.

John felt his son's head. "You are a little hot. Maybe you've caught a virus. Some soup will help. Any luck with the radio, Sam?" asked John.

Sam's curly blond hair peeked out from his plaid toque. He crouched on the ground as he moved the dials of the radio back and forth. He flipped the antenna up and down, but there was no sound.

"I've been fiddling with this radio for two hours," said Sam, "and I'm getting nothing. It's busted. Maybe it broke when we dropped it after the fog rolled in. Rob's right. We can't get in touch with anyone."

John sighed. "I wish we'd at least taken our compass on this sled trip, but in the rush to take off we left it back at the lodge. We were so sure this would be just a short, fun trip. But it's not turning out that way."

# 4

# Gloom and Doom

"We can't be far from the lodge, although it's possible we've been going in the opposite direction," said Sam. "You kids must be worried, and I bet your families are worried about you, too."

Emily nodded. "We don't know how far from home we are."

Matt could tell that Emily was being careful how she explained where they'd come from. They knew a group of scientists would never believe they flew in on a magic sled.

"And I bet you were stuck in that fog, too," said John.

"Yes. We were in a fog," said Matt.

"I wish those guides would show up. They know the land around here. They reassured us that they'd meet us. And now we can't even get in touch with them by radio," said Sam.

"We could be close to the lodge and not even know it," said Rob. "We could be stuck out here for days without enough food or water."

Matt shuddered. "Really?"

John patted Matt on the back. "We'll be fine. None of that is going to happen. Pay no attention to gloom-and-doom Rob. Sometimes I think he just likes to scare people. There are guides looking for us and we have enough food."

"For now. We have two extra mouths to feed, in case you've forgotten," said Rob.

John glared at Rob. "Let's stop worrying everybody. It doesn't help."

"I think we should set the tents up quickly, though," said Sam. "Those clouds look nasty. A storm is coming—and soon."

Just then the dogs began to howl.

"They also know a storm's on its way," said Sam.

"They're hungry and so am I," said John. "Some hot soup and stew will do us all good. Why don't you set the tents up and I'll start cooking the food and feeding the dogs."

"I could help make soup and stew," said Emily.

"Great. All you have to do is rip open some packets, add water, and stir the pot," said John.

Emily smiled. "I'm good at stirring pots, even when I'm not in the kitchen," she said. "My mom tells me that all the time."

John laughed. "You mean you're always up to some mischief, Emily?"

"A little—now and then," said Emily, smiling.

While Sam, Rob, and Matt pitched the tents, John fired up the camp stove and Emily added water to the food mix. She stirred the soup and stew till it was heated through.

"Mmmmm. It smells good," she said. "I love chicken noodle soup and beef stew."

"You must be really hungry to love this stuff," said John. "It's not gourmet food by any means." He glanced over at his son, who was sitting beside one of the tents.

"How are you feeling, Arthur?" John asked.

"Not so good, Dad. But I'll be okay."

John went over and patted Arthur on the back, then he headed off to feed the ten large dogs. He looked concerned.

"Do you want some soup, Arthur?" asked Emily.

Arthur shook his head. "I can't eat a thing, but don't tell my dad. He has enough to worry about already. I'm sure I'll feel better soon."

But despite his words, Emily and Matt could tell from the grimace on Arthur's face that he was feeling a lot worse than he'd admit.

# 5

# Moon Dog

"Look!" said Matt.

One of the dogs was barking and pulling at his rope. He looked like he wanted to head toward Arthur.

"That's Moon Dog," said Arthur. "He's a great dog."

"He's a great nuisance," said Rob. "He barks more than any other dog here, and he always wants you to pet him. What kind of sled dog is that? Our lead dog, Bruno, doesn't beg for attention every minute."

"Moon Dog and Arthur are good pals," John told Matt and Emily. "I think Moon Dog senses that Arthur isn't feeling well."

"Could you bring him over here, Dad?" Arthur asked.

"Don't do that," said Rob. "That dog's getting spoiled. Even if Moon Dog is not the lead dog, he's here to do a job. These are sled dogs. Not lap dogs for kids."

"Come on, Rob. Have a heart. My son isn't well."

"Look, I don't want your son to be sick, but I'm warning you about that dog. Don't complain to me if he doesn't perform when you treat him like a poodle in a queen's court," said Rob.

John shrugged and walked over to untie Moon Dog.

"Where did he get that name?" asked Matt.

"He was born during a full moon," said

Arthur as Moon Dog crouched beside him.

Arthur patted the big dog's head. Matt and Emily patted Moon Dog, too. Moon Dog licked Emily's hand.

"Moon Dog reminds me of Tiny," Emily whispered to Matt.

"Tiny and Moon Dog both like you, that's for sure," Matt whispered back.

"Having Moon Dog here makes me feel better," said Arthur.

Just then the wind began to howl, and snowflakes began to swirl around them.

"We'd better hurry inside. This storm is

kicking up quickly. Everybody grab some food and get into the tents," said John. "Matt, can you give me a hand with Arthur?"

"Sure," said Matt.

Matt and John helped Arthur stand up and hobble into the tent.

The snow was falling harder. The wind was churning up stronger and louder.

The kids helped Arthur off with his boots. Everyone huddled in the tents. Arthur, his father, Emily, and Matt shared the larger tent. Sam and Rob camped in the smaller one.

The tent shook as the wind slapped against it. "That wind sounds like a pack of hungry wolves," said John.

"I hope our sled is okay," said Matt. "I tied it to the tent pole."

"It should be fine. These are strong all-weather tents, and the poles are sturdy. I'm sure the wind will die down soon," said John. "Have some more soup. We all need to keep our strength up."

"Thanks for helping us. And thanks for the food," said Emily, sipping her soup. "I don't know what we would have done in this storm if we hadn't found you."

"Luckily this is a large tent, and you kids are dressed properly for the weather. We forgot our compass, but at least we brought two extra sleeping bags."

"Do you think the storm will blow over by morning?" said Arthur.

"I'm sure it will," said John. "And the guides are sure to find us with the morning light, too. Don't worry. Try and get some sleep."

Arthur closed his eyes. His breathing was heavy. His face was flushed, and sweat beaded on his forehead.

# 6

# Howls in the Night

John swallowed hard as he looked at his son. Emily and Matt knew that John was worried.

They were worried, too. What if the storm lasted for days? What if help didn't come in the morning? And how sick was Arthur? What if he was so sick that he needed a doctor?

Matt gulped. Suddenly he wasn't hungry. He put the soup down beside him on the ground.

"Finish your soup, Matt," said John. "Don't worry. We have enough food for at least another day. It might not be steak and french fries, but it will keep us going. I just hope Arthur's condition doesn't get worse."

"Maybe the dogs know the way to the lodge," said Matt, spooning up some more soup.

"If the guides don't find us in the morning, we'll have to rely on the dogs to show us the way. Our lead dog, Bruno, is tough and experienced. The guides promised us that in a pinch he'd take us to the lodge. But I didn't want to chance it in the dark and especially not in a storm. Let's try and get some sleep. We have a big day ahead of us."

Emily and Matt crawled into their sleeping bags with everything on except their boots. It felt strange sleeping in so many clothes. But it was cold and getting colder by the minute.

Soon, Arthur was breathing heavily and John was snoring loudly.

"He sounds like my dad," said Emily. "I can't sleep when someone is snoring like that. It sounds like a truck roaring down the highway."

"Well, I'm going to try to sleep," said Matt. He closed his eyes and was soon snoring softly.

But Emily couldn't sleep. She tossed and turned as the wind blew harder and fiercer and John snored louder and louder.

Then, over the wind, she heard howling and barking. She tapped Matt on the shoulder. "What's that?" she whispered.

Matt rubbed his eyes. "What's what?"

"That noise. It sounds like the dogs and some other animals."

Matt sat up. "You're right. It sounds like there's a fight going on."

"Let's peek outside and see."

"Are you sure that's a good idea? There could be wolves out there."

"We can just have a quick look. We don't have to go far. I can't sleep anyway," said Emily.

Emily and Matt slid out of their sleeping bags. They slipped on their boots and inched toward the flap of the tent. They lifted it up and peered out. There was a big snowdrift in front of their tent. They scooped snow away from the entrance with their hands. Then they crawled outside.

The snow and wind had slowed down but it was so dark, they could only see shadows. It was strangely quiet now, too.

"Maybe the fight is over," said Matt. But before he could say anything else, the barks and yelps started again. They were louder and fiercer than before.

Matt and Emily tried to see through the darkness, but they couldn't. Then the moon peeked through. In the dim light they could see

the dogs yanking at the ropes that held them
to the stakes in the snow.

"Look!" said Emily, pointing to a clearing
beside the trees. "Is that what I think it is?"

"Yes! It's a caribou, and it's running away
from some wolves," said Matt.

"But it's not running fast. I bet it's hurt. I
bet the wolves will get it. I can't look!"

# 7

# Where Is He?

Emily turned and hurried back into the tent. She covered her ears. She didn't want to hear the yelps, the howls, or the barking any longer. It sounded like the animals were ripping each other apart.

A few minutes later, Matt popped back inside, too. "Rob heard the noise and looked out. But the moon hid again and neither of us could see anything anymore," he said. "The wolves and caribou must have disappeared into the woods. But I bet that caribou is hurt—or worse."

Emily shivered. "Let's not think about it. We can't do anything to help that poor caribou. Let's try and sleep. It's quieter now outside, even though it's still noisy inside with all that snoring. I can't believe everyone else slept through all the animals barking and yelping outside."

Matt and Emily kicked off their boots and crawled back into their sleeping bags.

"At least it's cozy in here," Emily whispered as she snuggled into the sleeping bag. "And I'm so tired. Goodnight, Matt."

But Matt didn't answer. He'd fallen asleep as soon as he slid back into his sleeping bag.

Soon, despite the snoring, so did Emily.

The next thing the friends heard was a booming voice shouting, "Where is he?"

"Where is who?" asked Emily, opening her eyes.

"Is it morning already?" asked Matt, yawning and stretching. "I feel like I've only been asleep for five minutes."

"What are we supposed to do now?" shouted the person again.

"Where's John?" asked Matt, looking around the tent.

"And Arthur?" asked Emily.

The friends slid out of their sleeping bags and pulled on their boots. They lifted the tent's flap. Someone had dug a real path through the snow. Emily and Matt stepped outside.

The snow was piled high everywhere. It covered the sleds, the hills, the trees, and the tops of the tents. Everything was white except the sky. The sun was starting to poke through the clouds.

Emily and Matt hurried over to the group. John and Rob were cleaning off the sleds, while Sam was crouched down, picking up some wrappers from their food that were strewn in the snow. Arthur lay down in a sled, bundled up in layers of clothes.

"Bruno was our only hope," said Rob. "The guides said he was the best dog to lead us back. And now he's gone. How did he get untied? Where did he go?"

"Calm down, Rob," said John. "He may come back. And we have other dogs."

"What happened?" asked Emily.

"Bruno has disappeared," said Sam. "We were counting on him to lead us if we needed help returning to the lodge, and we do. He must have gotten loose last night. Rob says there were wolves and caribou around here. We saw tracks in the snow this morning."

"We saw the caribou and the wolves last night. After everyone went to sleep, we heard noises. So we peeked out and saw the caribou being chased by some wolves. But we didn't see Bruno take off," said Emily.

"Maybe his rope was loose or he yanked himself free. He could be anywhere now," said Sam.

"Or dead," said Rob.

"We have to forget about Bruno now. The clouds are thickening. We may be in for more snow. Let's ready the sleds with Moon Dog in the lead," said John.

"That pooch is a pussy cat. Not a dog. We'll have to stop and pet him every few minutes," said Rob. "Look at him. He's licking your son's hand, John. How can we rely on a dog like that?"

# 8

# Mush

"We have to rely on Moon Dog," said John. "Come on, Matt. Help me check on our supplies. Then we can pack up and go."

John and Matt ran toward a spot behind the tents. "Look!" said Matt.

"Oh no. I don't believe this," said John.

A pole was lying on the ground. There was no sign of the supplies that had been hung from it.

Matt and John looked everywhere for the supplies. But they only found a few bits of food scattered in the snow.

"It's all gone!" cried John.

"What's gone?" asked Rob as John and Matt hurried back to the group.

"Some animal has gotten into our supplies. I packed everything up carefully last night. At least I thought I did. I stored it all high on two poles. The wind probably knocked one pole down in the storm. And now the food has been devoured by animals."

Rob rolled his eyes. "What else is going to go wrong? This trip is turning into a nightmare."

John took a deep breath. "I'm sorry about this."

"It's nobody's fault," said Sam. "We have to get out of here fast. That's all. And we have to trust our remaining dogs, especially Moon Dog. We have no choice."

"Moon Dog will get us back. You'll see," said Arthur.

"Are you feeling any better, Arthur?" asked Matt.

"Not much, but I'll be okay."

Matt glanced at Emily. They both knew that Arthur was still trying to act brave so no one would worry.

"How much food is left?" asked Rob.

"A little soup. Some trail mix. Water," said John. "We should be fine for a day or so. Let's get going. That's all we can do."

They all helped pack up the tents. As they loaded the three sleds, it began to snow again. John stood behind Moon Dog's lead sled.

Matt squished into Rob's large sled with Emily, the magic sled, and a load of supplies. Sam stood behind his smaller sled.

They were ready.

John rubbed his son's back.

"It's not going to be an easy ride, Arthur,"

he said. "The ground will be bumpy even with the snow."

"I'll be okay, Dad," said Arthur. "Don't worry."

"Then let's mush," said John. He yanked the reins, signalling the dogs to run.

Moon Dog took off like a shot.

"Well, he's certainly enthusiastic," called Sam, as he and his dogs followed John's sled.

"But for what?" called Rob. "He could just be taking us on a wild ride into nowhere."

"Let's think good thoughts," Emily said. Rob rolled his eyes.

"Oh, no! Look!" Rob slowed his dogs down. "Poor beast!" he said, pointing to a spot near the trees. John and Sam slowed their sleds and looked back. They all stared at what remained of a dead caribou.

Emily gulped. "It was probably the one the wolves attacked last night," she murmured.

Sam shook his head "Not much is left of that creature after those wolves had their fill. Maybe the caribou was already hurt. Wolves will attack the weakest caribou. We certainly saw that when we followed the herds."

"But where's Bruno?" asked Rob.

"I hope he survived meeting the wolves," said Matt.

"Let's go," said John. "There's nothing we can do here." He signalled his dogs to mush.

For the next hour no one said anything. The dogs panted as they flew across the swirling snow.

Then Moon Dog started barking.

He stopped running.

# 9

# Gone Crazy

"Come on, Moon Dog. Mush!" said John.

But Moon Dog refused to budge. He barked and barked.

"Has he gone crazy? I told you this dog doesn't know what he's doing or where he's going. Why is he stopping here?" asked Rob.

"He hasn't gone crazy," said Emily. "I think he was limping!"

John hopped off the sled and hurried over to Moon Dog. "You're right, Emily. There's a piece of a pine needle stuck in his paw. That can hurt like crazy. Let me see if I can get it out."

Everyone waited as John bent over Moon Dog. "Got it!" he said. "He should be fine now. Ready, Moon Dog?"

Moon Dog gave a quick wag of his tail.

But before all the sleds took off, Sam pointed to a clump of bushes under a thin blanket of snow. "Cloudberries!" he said. "I wouldn't mind a handful of those."

Everyone except Arthur hopped off the sleds. They picked cloudberries off the bushes.

Matt popped some into his mouth first. Then he scrunched up his nose. "These are sour," he said.

"They make great jam," said Sam, smiling. "But they are a little hard to love uncooked."

"They make my eyes water," said Emily.

"They're good for you and they grow in the cold," said Sam.

After everyone had eaten a few handfuls of berries, John said, "Let's go."

He stepped back on his sled. Everyone else jumped on their sleds, too.

"Mush, Moon Dog!" said John. Moon Dog raced across the snow. The rest of the dogs and sleds followed.

Emily and Matt looked for signs of a lodge as they bounced across the snow-covered ground. But they couldn't see anything except the snow falling around them. They sledded on and on. They seemed to be sledding for hours, but there was still no sign of a lodge or people.

Finally John signalled for the sleds to stop. "Let's have some soup and give the dogs a rest," he said. "It's late afternoon already."

Emily and Matt hopped off their sled. They

hurried over to Arthur. His face was flushed. He took deep breaths and held his stomach. He seemed to be getting sicker by the minute.

"Are you queasy?" his father asked.

Arthur nodded.

"I hope it's not his appendix," said Rob. "If it is, this is a real emergency."

John took a deep breath. "We'll eat something quickly and keep moving. That's all we can do."

Everyone ate a bowl of hot soup except Arthur, who could only manage to sip some water.

"We don't have much daylight left," Emily whispered to Matt.

"I know. I hope we're not going to have to sleep in the tents again," Matt whispered back.

Matt and Emily looked at the others in the group. The look on each man's face as he peered up at the sky was the same.

The adults were worried, too.

# 10

# A Tumble in the Snow

"Mush!" said John, and Moon Dog and the other dogs took off again. For a few minutes the sleds flew over the snow. Then Moon Dog slipped. His legs buckled as he fell into a drop in the ground. He tumbled into a snowbank.

"Ow," groaned Arthur as John and Arthur fell into a snowbank, too.

The other sleds stopped. Everyone hurried to help.

"Are you hurt?" asked Matt.

"I'm okay, and so is Arthur," said John,

shaking the snow off his parka and pants. "Luckily, Arthur fell into soft snow and on top of his thick blanket. But it looks like Moon Dog sprained his leg."

"What do we do now?" asked Rob.

"Help me lift the sled up and put Arthur back in," said John. Sam, Rob, Matt, and Emily helped lift the sled and then placed Arthur gently back into the sled.

"I'm going to wrap Moon Dog's leg and see if he can still walk," said John.

"I thought sled dogs had more sense than to trip," said Rob.

"It was an accident. He couldn't see the dip in the ground," said Emily. "See how good he is about getting bandaged?"

It was true. Moon Dog didn't bark or wiggle. He stood there patiently, waiting for John to finish.

"Moon Dog knows that we're trying to help him," said Matt. "And he knows we need his help, too."

"Okay. I admit it, kids. That dog may not have a clue where he's going, but he's not a whiner," said Rob.

"Let's see if he can walk," said John.

Everyone watched as Moon Dog took a wobbly step. Then another and another. After taking a few more uncertain steps, he sprinted toward Arthur and licked his hand.

Arthur smiled weakly and patted Moon Dog's head.

"Moon Dog is amazing," said Matt.

"Maybe he can still lead us," said Emily.

"He's certainly helping Arthur," said John. "You're right, Emily. Maybe he can lead us. Maybe not as fast as before, but let's see. Everyone, take your places in your sleds."

John hitched Moon Dog back up and everyone in the group returned to their sleds.

"Mush, Moon Dog," said John.

Moon Dog took a step. Then another. And another. Then he began to race across the snow. All the dogs and sleds followed.

Soon there was little daylight left. They'd have to stop and set up the tents. But Arthur was so sick. How would he get through another night without a doctor?

Suddenly, they heard a loud *pop*. The sleds came to a stop.

"Was that a gun? Are there hunters around here?" said Sam.

"We'd better be careful. We don't want them to shoot us by accident," said Rob.

"At least there are people around here somewhere," said John. "I'll fire a shot into the air, too. Then we should call out to them."

The far-off gunshots sounded again.

John fired his gun into the air. Everyone in the group called for help. The dogs barked and pulled at the reins.

*Boom. Boom. Boom.* More gunshots in the distance.

This time louder. Closer.

"Why don't they stop shooting? Can't they hear us?" said Sam.

"I'm firing again. After that, yell as loud as you can!" said John.

John fired into the air. Everyone shouted.

"Look. Over there!" cried Emily.

Two men on snowmobiles were coming toward them over a small hill. They were waving and calling.

"Phew," said John, taking a deep breath and leaning against the sled.

"Dad," said Arthur, "I'm going to throw up." And he did.

# 11

# Wrong

The men got off their snowmobiles and ran over. They were the group's Inuit guides!

"We've been looking for you all day," said one of the guides, who introduced himself to Emily and Matt as Len. "We shot the guns in the air to signal you."

"We thought you were hunters. Thank goodness you found us," said John, grasping each man's hand. "We are so glad to see you!"

"We would have found you yesterday as we'd arranged," said the other guide, whose name was Kevin, "but the snowstorm came up so quickly and unexpectedly from the north that it wasn't safe to travel. We couldn't see anything. We knew you had tents, food, and a radio, so we counted on you to be okay till the storm ended."

"We might have been if our radio hadn't gone bust," said Sam.

"And if we hadn't lost most of our food," said Rob.

"And if we didn't have a sick kid," said John. "How far are we from the lodge?"

"You're only five minutes away. It's behind those trees to the south. Moon Dog led you to safety," Kevin explained.

"Well, I'll be..." said Rob, smiling for the first time since they'd started sledding. "Moon Dog knew where he was going. I guess you kids were right to believe in him after all."

Moon Dog licked Rob's hand as if he understood what the man was saying. "Cut it out," said Rob, pushing Moon Dog away. "I don't like you *that* much."

Everyone laughed.

"Arthur needs help fast," said John. "He's really sick."

"There's a doctor on an ice fishing trip who's staying at the lodge," said Len. "He should be able to help your son. Follow us."

Everyone hurried back to their sleds and followed the guides to the lodge. Just as they said, it was only a five-minute ride away.

The minute they arrived, the guides found the doctor. While he examined Arthur, Emily sketched Moon Dog, who was tied up outside the lodge with the other dogs. Moon Dog paced back and forth.

"I have to record this," said Matt, turning on his recorder. "We've had a wild Arctic adventure," said Matt. "We met scientists studying wolves and caribou, got caught in a snowstorm, and were saved by a smart sled dog named Moon Dog. We're waiting to hear about our friend, Arthur. Moon Dog is waiting, too. He's worried about Arthur just like we are. He's an awesome dog."

Matt flipped the recorder off as John ran outside.

"I know you kids would want to hear about Arthur," said John. "It looks like he has appendicitis. But in ten minutes, we're taking a floatplane to Yellowknife, where he'll be seen in a hospital. He may have to have an operation, but he'll be fine. He wanted to tell you kids thanks and goodbye."

"Tell him we hope he's better soon!" said Matt.

"I will," said John. "And guess who else showed up here? Bruno! He limped back an hour ago with a cut leg and deep scratches on his face. But he'll be fine. He must have gotten into a tussle with those wolves."

"Wow!" said Emily. "I'm glad he's okay. I'm glad we're all okay."

"But your family doesn't know that. I bet they're at the lodge by now. It's packed with groups from dogsled adventures. So go find

them. They must be frantic about you."

With that, John waved and hurried back inside.

"We *are* going to see our family," said Emily. "Look at the sled."

Shimmering gold words were forming at the front of their magic sled.

*You flew up north.*
*You raced on snow.*
*But now it's time*
*For you to go.*

Emily and Matt hopped on their sled. Instantly, it flew up.

Soon they were soaring over the lodge, over the snow-covered ground, and into a fluffy white cloud.

When they landed in Emily's tower, they hopped off.

"I'm glad that Arthur will be all right," said Emily. "It must have been awful being so sick and riding on a bumpy sled. It was wobblier than I thought it would be."

"And Rob was grumpy all the way. I wish we'd been riding with Sam instead of him. He kept saying mean things under his breath about Moon Dog. Boy, was he wrong."

"Well, at least he admitted he was wrong. Wasn't that an amazing adventure?"

"It was awesome, but it made me really hungry," said Matt.

"I didn't like those sour cloudberries very much. How about a bowl of better berries?"

"What kind do you have?"

"Sugar berries," said Emily.

"I've never heard of sugar berries. Where do they come from?"

Emily laughed. "They come from my

cupboard and my fridge. All you have to do is get a bowl of blueberries or strawberries and add some sugar. If the berries are sour, that makes them extra sweet. And then you have sugar berries. It's easy and yummy. Want some?"

Matt smiled. "Yes. Your sugar berries sound delicious."

"Then let's mush into the kitchen!" said Emily.

And they did.

# MORE ABOUT...

After their adventure, Matt and Emily wanted to know more about dogsledding, wolves, caribou, and the North. Turn the page for their favourite facts.

# Matt's Top Ten Facts

1. Wolves look like big husky dogs. In Canada, the largest wolves are found in the northwest part of the country and the smallest ones live on the Arctic islands.

2. Wolves mark their territory with the scent of their you—know—what.

   *The scent is pee, right? —E.*

3. Wolf pups are born blind and deaf.

4. Wolves' thick coats are often grey, but can also be white or black, or a mixture of colours. White wolves are common in the Arctic.

5. Wolves hunt and eat in groups called packs. They often eat caribou.

6. Wolves love to howl. The leader of the wolf pack usually howls loudest.

7. Here are some other wild animals beside caribou and wolves that roam around the Northwest Territories: moose, Dall sheep, elk, snowshoe hares, wolverines, and Arctic foxes.

8. Sometimes cloudberries are called baked apple berries. They don't look like apples but some people say they taste like honeyed apples. They're expensive because they don't grow in many places.

9. If you want to stay warm and comfortable while camping in winter, wear layers of clothing.

10. Don't eat snow! It's not healthy for you. Snow contains a lot of bacteria and pesticides that can make you sick.

# Emily's Top Ten Facts

**1.** In 2001, the Canadian Inuit dog became Nunavut's official mammal. The Inuit call them "qimmiq."

**2.** The Canadian Inuit dog was honoured with a stamp in 1988 and a fifty-cent coin in 1997.

*I call them frisky and friendly.*
*—M.*

**3.** Dogsled racing is popular in the Northwest Territories. Sled-racing dogs have to be fast and tough. They often travel an average of 32 km (20 miles) an hour.

**4.** Here are some northern dogs used in sledding: Alaskan Husky, Alaskan Malamute, Canadian Inuit dog, Chinook, Labrador Husky, and Siberian Husky.

**5.** Sled dogs have a good sense of direction and can see farther than humans.

*And they never need glasses.*
*—M.*

**6.** Joseph-Armand Bombardier from Quebec designed the first modern snowmobile in 1958. He called it a Ski-Do.

**7.** Caribou can usually outrun wolves unless they are injured or the wolves attack them by surprise.

They run as fast as a car drives in the country —M.

**8.** Caribou have always been an important source of food for Canada's northern people but they are now endangered.

**9.** In the 1970s, scientists usually counted caribou by watching them. Today scientists often track caribou by taking photographs of them from the air.

**10.** In 1974 scientist counted 251,000 Bathurst caribou. In 2009 only 32,000 were counted.

# So You Want to Know...

## FROM AUTHOR FRIEDA WISHINSKY

When I was writing this book, my friends wanted to know more about dogsledding and the Northern environment. I told them that although all the characters in this story are made up, the story is based on my research on dogsledding, climate change, caribou, wolves, and the Northwest Territories.

Here are some questions I answered:

**When did people start using dogs for sledding?**

No one knows exactly when humans began to use dogs for sledding, but archaeologists have found evidence that the Thule people were probably the first to use dogs around 1000 CE. Dogsledding is also mentioned in Arabian literature. It describes dogs being used in the Siberian Arctic in the tenth century.

In his writings at the end of the thirteenth century, the explorer Marco Polo mentions dogsleds; and in a 1675 edition of explorer Martin Frobisher's book *Historic Navigations*, there's an illustration of a dog pulling a canoe-like sled. In the seventeenth and eighteenth centuries, dogsledding became popular for trade and travel with the early colonists and voyageurs in Canada's New France.

## What jobs did sled dogs do?

Sled dogs helped traders, hunters, and fishermen with their work. They were used to deliver mail, supplies, and news to remote places. In the 1870s, the North West Mounted Police used sled dogs to patrol the Canadian wilderness.

## How and why were dogsleds involved in exploring the North and South Pole?

Sled dogs are good for travelling on ice and snow. They're also intelligent and strong. That's why Arctic explorers used them to reach the poles. Admiral Peary used 133 dogs in his race to be first to the North Pole. Roald Amundsen used dogs in his bid to be first to the South Pole. But Amundsen's rival explorer Robert

Scott didn't have confidence in dogs and relied instead on horses on his South Pole expedition. Many people believe that was one of the reasons that Scott's expedition failed to reach the Pole first, and that Scott and his men died on their way back from the Pole.

**Have sled dogs rescued people in distress?**

There's a famous sled-dog rescue story that happened in 1925. That year, there was an outbreak of a terrible disease called diphtheria in Nome, Alaska. The only serum to fight the disease was in Anchorage, Alaska, more than 1,500 km (930 miles) away. There were no aircraft available, so a sled-dog team was used to transport the serum. The lead dog for the last leg of the journey was named Balto. He led the team through dangerous whiteout conditions and delivered the serum to Nome. Many lives were saved. The newspapers reported the story, and later a statue of Balto was erected in New York's Central Park.

**How has the snowmobile changed the way sled dogs are used today?**

These days, people don't rely as much on sled dogs for survival in the North because of the popularity of snowmobiles. But there are still many people who enjoy dogsledding for leisure and for sport.

## Why do scientists think that the caribou population has been reduced in recent years?

Scientists think that modern hunting equipment, like snowmobiles, has contributed to killing many more caribou. They also believe that companies exploring for oil and gas and mining diamonds in the Arctic have destroyed the caribou's natural habitat. And on top of that, global warming has made it increasingly difficult for the caribou to find food.

## What does "global warming" mean?

The term "global warming" was first used in a scientific paper in 1975. It means that the Earth's average surface temperature is increasing. Oceans are also warming up and sea levels are rising. Glaciers are melting faster than ever before.

## What's causing global warming?

Scientists say that burning fossil fuels such as coal and petroleum allows greenhouse gases like carbon dioxide to escape into the air. These gases cause most of the warming. Cutting down forests also increases global warming because trees soak up carbon dioxide from the air.

## What can people do about slowing down global warming?

We can encourage governments to burn less fossil fuel and use better-for-the-environment sources of energy like solar or wind power. We can encourage governments not to destroy forests. We can also use less energy in our daily lives. For example, we can turn lights off when we don't need them and walk more instead of driving cars. We can also buy food that's been grown locally. Local food is usually fresher and doesn't need to be transported long distances.

Coming next in the
*Canadian Flyer Adventures* Series...

# Canadian Flyer Adventures
# #17

# Halifax
# Explodes!

Emily and Matt land in Halifax, just after the
fateful blast in 1917.

For a sneak peek at the latest book in the series, visit:
**www.owlkids.com**
and click on the red maple leaf!

# The *Canadian Flyer Adventures* Series

**#1 Beware, Pirates!**

**#2 Danger, Dinosaurs!**

**#3 Crazy for Gold**

**#4 Yikes, Vikings!**

**#5 Flying High!**

**#6 Pioneer Kids**

**#7 Hurry, Freedom**

**#8 A Whale Tale**

**#9 All Aboard!**

**#10 Lost in the Snow**

**#11 Far from Home**

**#12 On the Case**

**#13 Stop that Stagecoach!**

**#14 SOS! Titanic!**

**#15 Make It Fair!**

**#16 Arctic Storm**

## Upcoming Book

Look out for the next book that will take Emily and Matt on a new adventure:

## #17 Halifax Explodes!

# More Praise for the Series

"[Emily and Matt] learn more than they ever could have from a history textbook. Every book in this new series promises to shed light on a different chapter of Canadian history."
~ *MONTREAL GAZETTE*

"Readers are in for a great adventure."
~ *EDMONTON'S CHILD*

"This series makes Canadian history fun, exciting and accessible."
~ *CHRONICLE HERALD (HALIFAX)*

"[An] enthralling series for junior-school readers."
~ *HAMILTON SPECTATOR*

"...highly entertaining, very educational but not too challenging. A terrific new series."
~ *RESOURCE LINKS*

"This wonderful new Canadian historical adventure series combines magic and history to whisk young readers away on adventure...A fun way to learn about Canada's past."
~ *BC PARENT*

"Highly recommended."
~ *CM: CANADIAN REVIEW OF MATERIALS*

Teacher Resource Guides now available online. Please visit our website at
**www.owlkids.com**
and click on the red maple leaf to download tips and ideas for using the series in the classroom.

# About the Author

Frieda Wishinsky, a former teacher, is an award-winning picture- and chapter-book author, who has written many beloved and bestselling books for children. Frieda enjoys using humour and history in her work, while exploring new ways to tell a story. Her books have earned much critical praise, including a nomination for a Governor General's Literary Award. She is the author of *Please, Louise; You're Mean, Lily Jean; Each One Special;* and *What's the Matter with Albert?* among others. Originally from New York, Frieda now lives in Toronto.

# About the Illustrator

Patricia Ann Lewis-MacDougall started drawing as soon as she could hold a pencil, and filled every blank spot in her mother's cookbooks by the age of three. As she grew up, Pat Ann never stopped drawing and enjoyed learning all about the worlds of animation and illustration. She now tells stories with her love of drawing and has illustrated children's books and created storyboards for television animation for shows such as *Little Bear* and *Franklin the Turtle*. Pat Ann lives in Stoney Creek, Ontario.